ONE WAY

ADOPT A DOG TODAY!

I LO♥E Dogs!

By Sue Stainton and Bob Staake

KATHERINE TEGEN BOOKS
An Imprint of HarperCollins Publishers

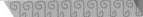

Katherine Tegen Books
is an imprint of HarperCollins Publishers.
I Love Dogs!
Text copyright © 2014 by Sue Stainton
Illustrations copyright © 2014 by Bob Staake

ISBN 978-0-06-117057-7

The artist used Adobe Photoshop 3.0 to create the digital illustrations for this book.
Typography by Jeanne L. Hogle   14 15 16 17 18 SCP   10 9 8 7 6 5 4 3 2 1 ❖   First Edition

To Mum and Dad
—S.S.

To every cat that secretly wished
they'd been born a dog
—B.S.

ADOPT
A DOG
TODAY!

Dogs,
dogs,
dogs.

I love dogs!

Strong dogs,

long dogs.

Nosy dogs,

cozy dogs.

ADOPT A DOG TODAY! →

Lazy dogs,

crazy dogs.

Chasing dogs,

racing dogs.

Speedy dogs,

greedy dogs.

Dogs in the snow,

dogs that know.

I
love
dogs!

Dogs, dogs, dogs.

I love dogs!

Spotty dogs,

dotty dogs.

Wrinkly dogs,

crinkly dogs.

ADOPT A DOG TODAY!

Yappy dogs,

happy dogs.

Fluffy dogs,

scruffy dogs.

Prowling dogs,

howling dogs.

ADOPT
A DOG
TODAY!

Dogs in the park,
dogs that bark.

I love dogs!

ADOPT
A DOG
TODAY! →

Dogs, dogs, dogs.
I love dogs!

Curly dogs,

burly dogs.

Hairy dogs,

scary dogs.

Naughty dogs,

haughty dogs.

ADOPT A DOG TODAY! →

Shaggy dogs,

waggy dogs.

Trendy dogs,

bendy dogs.

Sniffy dogs,

whiffy dogs.

Dogs that are famous,
dogs that are smart.
Dogs in the news,
dogs in fine art.

Dogs that wag tails,
dogs that chew bones.
Dogs in big houses,
dogs without homes.

Dogs, dogs, dogs.
I love dogs!